810.8
J135p

MW00335703

+810.8
J135p

JACKSON
PIRATES, SHIPS, AND SAILORS

8.06

SPARTA FREE LIBRARY
608-269-2010

DEMCO

SPARTA FREE LIBRARY
P.O. Box 347
Sparta, WI 54656

Pirates, Ships, AND Sailors

By Kathryn and Byron Jackson
Illustrated by Gustaf Tenggren

SPARTA FREE LIBRARY
P.O. Box 347
Sparta, WI 54656

A GOLDEN BOOK · NEW YORK

Copyright © 1950 by Random House, Inc. All rights reserved under International and Pan-American Copyright Conventions.
Published in the United States by Golden Books, an imprint of Random House Children's Books, a division of Random House,
Inc., New York, and simultaneously in Canada by Random House of Canada Limited, Toronto. Originally published in 1950
in slightly different form by Simon & Schuster, Inc., and Artists and Writers Guild, Inc. Golden Books, A Golden Book, and
the G colophon are registered trademarks of Random House, Inc.
Library of Congress Cataloging-in-Publication Data
Jackson, Kathryn.
Pirates, ships, and sailors / by Kathryn and Byron Jackson ; illustrated by Gustaf Tenggren.
p. cm.
Summary: Features a collection of sea stories and poems with tales of treasure chests, stowaways,
sea serpents, sea captains, and pirates.
ISBN: 0-375-83665-9   ISBN: 0-375-93665-3 (lib. bdg.)
1. Sea stories, American. 2. Children's stories, American. 3. Seafaring life—Juvenile poetry.
4. Children's poetry, American. [1. Sea stories. 2. Short stories. 3. Seafaring life—Poetry. 4. American poetry.]
I. Jackson, Byron, 1899–1949. II. Tenggren, Gustaf, 1806–1970, ill. III. Title.
PZ7.J13625Pi 2006
[Fic]—dc22   2005015513
www.goldenbooks.com
www.randomhouse.com/kids
Educators and librarians, for a variety of teaching tools, visit us at
www.randomhouse.com/teachers
PRINTED IN CHINA   10 9 8 7 6 5 4 3 2 1

CONTENTS

PIRATE'S COVE

Pirate's Cove was a wonderful place to live in during the summer. There was the bright sea for a boy to swim in, and the curved white beach shaped like a brand-new moon. There were the cliffs, and the rolling hills to play on and explore.

Best of all, there was the name Pirate's Cove.

Pirate's Cove! Kit could close his eyes and see a great pirate schooner rocking in the harbor. He could see its black flag blowing against the blue sky. Sometimes he could even see a band of pirates coming ashore. They rowed in, shouting and singing, with their peg legs, and eye patches, and a heavy chest of treasure to hide at the Cove.

And who knew—perhaps the pirate treasure was still there! Who knew—maybe a boy could find it!

"If he searched long enough, and dug deeply enough," thought Kit, "maybe a boy my size could find a chest full of old pirate gold!"

Kit even thought the boy might be himself! So he got a shovel for digging and he took his flashlight for looking in holes. And he took a chocolate bar, in case of sudden hunger.

Then Kit went out, and every day he dug in a different place.

He dug under trees that looked like good landmarks. He dug holes in the beach, and at the edge of the cranberry bog. He dug in likely places and unlikely places.

And one day Kit dug up a rusty lantern. He ran home with that.

"Does it look like a pirate's lantern?" he asked his father.

"No," said his father. "It looks like it might be an eel fisherman's lantern."

That's what it was. It belonged to old Silas Prentiss, who was glad to get it back. And one day Kit found a skull.

"Does it look like a pirate's skull?" he asked his father.

"No, it doesn't, Kit," his father said. "It looks exactly like a sheep's skull."

Then he said, "You know, Kit, pirates roved the sea over a hundred and fifty years ago, and I think you're wasting your time. I think you'd be better off learning the crawl or rowing your boat."

"Is that orders," asked Kit, "or is it up to me?"

"It's up to you, Kit," his father said. "But I'd like to see you playing on the beach."

The next day, Kit practiced his crawl. He rowed his boat up the Cove. The water sparkled. The sunshine was warm on his head.

"My father was right," he thought. "This is fun. I like this."

He watched a seagull soar lazily toward the hill. Its shadow slid across the beach, then along the cliff. Suddenly the shadow disappeared. Kit looked sharply at the cliff. There was a hole in it, right where it met the water. A hole like the door of a cave.

Kit swung his boat toward the beach. He rowed to shore and dropped overboard the big stone he used for an anchor. He ran across the beach and waded along the face of the cliff to the cave.

Kit's heart was beating as loudly as the sea. He peeped into the cave. It smelled of seaweed, and damp, and salt. It was dark in there. Kit turned on his flashlight and crept in. The cave was big inside. He could stand up.

"Even a pirate could stand up in here," he thought. And when he thought "pirate," he was sure this was the hiding place. There were rocks all about, damp rocks that shone in the flashlight beam.

One by one, Kit moved those rocks. But there was no hole under any of them. So he walked around the cave, searching the walls.

At last he found a loose rock. He pried it with his knife, and it came out. Kit reached into the hole.

"There's something in it!" he shouted.

"—in it!" called a hollow voice back in the cave.

Kit jumped—then laughed a shaky laugh. The voice was only an echo!

He reached into the hole and brought out a rusty box.

"It's a mighty small box for a treasure," he thought.

He opened the creaking lid. Oh, gosh, there was no ruby in it, no big perfect pearl, not even a very small diamond!

There was a paper in it. A folded, heavy piece of paper.

Kit took it out into the sunshine. At first it looked blank, the sunshine was so bright. But then Kit could see lines and numbers and letters on it.

"A map," he whispered. "It's a treasure map!"

It didn't take Kit long to get home. He found his father under the car talking to himself. Kit wriggled under, too.

"Look, Daddy," he said. "Look at this! Does it look like a pirate's map?"

"Pirates!" his father growled. "Here, hold this wrench, Kit."

At last his father said, "There, I have that leak fixed."

He shoved himself out from under the car and sat on the grass. Kit flopped down beside him and gave him the paper.

His father looked at it and whistled. Then he shook his head and frowned.

"Kit," he said, "somebody's teasing you. Everybody in the Cove knows you're treasure hunting. Somebody hid that map for you to find."

Kit gulped.

"Are you sure, Daddy?" he asked. "Are you certain it isn't a pirate's map?"

Kit's father nodded.

"I'm sure," he said. "Look, it says, 'From the bent tree, a hundred paces due east in line with the turtle back—'"

"Yes, I see," Kit said. "What's wrong with that? What's a turtle back?"

"It's the island with the lighthouse on it," Kit's father said. "It looked like a turtle before they built the lighthouse."

He pointed to the old tree that leaned over the cliff.

"You see, Kit, if you went a hundred paces from the tree—you'd be out in deep water."

"Oh," sighed Kit. He sounded like air going out of a balloon.

His father patted his shoulder.

"Never mind, Kit," he said. "When I get the car running I'll take you down to the post office. We might stop for a soda, too."

"Yes, sir," Kit said. "First I'd better get my flashlight. I left it in the cave."

But once he was in his boat, Kit could not go straight to the cave. He looked up at the bent tree, and he looked out at the lighthouse on the turtle back.

He rowed his boat in a straight line between the two. And every few feet Kit stopped and looked down into the clear water of the Cove.

He saw little snappers darting into the shadows. He saw an eel and a horseshoe crab. He saw the green seaweed waving on the white bottom of the Cove.

And then all at once, Kit saw a place where the white bottom did not show. It looked like a shadow. Kit's small head could not make a shadow that big. Kit leaned way over the side and looked down.

He leaned a bit too far, and the boat tipped, and Kit fell into the water with a great splash.

"Ugh!" spluttered Kit when he came up.

Then he laughed at himself.

"Pretty clumsy, pretty clumsy! But now that I'm in here, I'm going to see what that dark patch is on the bottom!"

He swam down as far as he could, and he looked still farther down. There was a big green rock down there. There was something else.

It looked like a boat. It looked like a funny kind of boat. Just what kind, Kit could not see. He had to go up for air.

When he came up, his small boat had drifted away. Kit started to swim for it. But somebody called, "Hello, Kit!"

It was his father. He was coming toward the boy in his motorboat.

In a few seconds, Kit was beside his father in the launch.

"I said practice your crawl," his father said sternly, "but I didn't say, 'See if you can swim to Spain'!"

12

"I fell out of my boat," Kit panted. "I was looking at a hundred paces due east, and Daddy, there's a boat down there—it's a funny boat—"

Just then Kit remembered his own boat. It was drifting out toward the sea.

"Look, Daddy!" he shouted. "It will get lost!"

It didn't take long for the motorboat to catch Kit's rowboat. Kit jumped into the water again and tied the rowboat to the stern of his father's boat. His father swung him aboard.

"Can we look at that sunken boat, Daddy?" he asked eagerly.

"You just bet we can," his father said. He spun the wheel. Kit pointed the way.

Together the two leaned over the side and looked down at the green shadow.

"Does it look like a pirate dinghy?" Kit whispered.

His father did not answer. He was kicking off his shoes. He grabbed a rope and put it around his waist. Then he dived down into the clear water.

When he came up, Kit asked again, "Does it, Daddy?"

His father took a deep breath. "Thought we could tow the boat ashore. But the wood is rotten. The boat has been there too long."

"Has it been there a hundred and fifty years?" Kit asked eagerly.

"Maybe it has," his father said.

Then he dived down a second time. When he bobbed up again, he flung the end of the rope to Kit, and climbed into the boat.

"We'll soon see, Kit," said his father.

He pulled and pulled on that long rope. Pretty soon Kit could see a dark shape coming up through the water. It was squarish. It looked green. It looked like a large box all green from being in the water.

Kit did not ask any questions now. His father reached into the water and lifted the dripping box into the boat.

"It's light, Kit," he said. "It's too light to have much in it."

He put his knife under the rusted lock and broke it open. Together Kit and his father looked in. A hole had rusted in the bottom of the box.

"Whatever *was* in it is gone now," Kit's father said. Now *his* voice sounded like an emptying balloon.

But Kit reached into a corner of the box.

"Look, Daddy!" He held up an old darkened coin.

His father felt and looked at it, and rubbed it in the sand in the bottom of the boat.

"It's a gold coin, Kit!" he shouted.

And before Kit could say one word, his father had dived into the water again.

At last he came up, panting hard and dripping.

"There's nothing else down there," he said.

He picked up the one gold coin and turned it over and over in his hand. Then he gave it to Kit.

"Well, Kit," he said. "There's your pirate treasure. The rest has long ago been washed out to sea. Not a chance of finding any more of it."

"Is it *really* pirate gold?" Kit asked.

His father nodded.

"Sure enough," he said. "It's a real Spanish doubloon. That old box must have been full of them at one time. It's a pirate's treasure chest, certain sure."

Kit looked at his wonderful Spanish doubloon. He looked out at the shining water.

"A hundred paces due east," he whispered happily.

So the big pirate schooner really had anchored in the Cove, and the pirates really had rowed toward shore with their peg legs and eye patches, and a big chest of treasure to hide at the Cove!

Yes, Pirate's Cove was a wonderful place to live in during the summer. Pirate's Cove! Who knew—maybe there was more treasure somewhere? So much that the pirates had not bothered to bring up the small chest in the dinghy boat that sank. And who knew—maybe a small boy might find it.

"A boy just my size," Kit murmured.

"A boy just your size had better get on some dry clothes if he wants to go to the village with me," his father said.

And side by side, both dripping wet, they rode slowly in toward the curved white beach that was shaped like a brand-new moon.

STOWAWAY JUDY

Judy watched the seven trim sailboats practicing for the big race. All of them looked beautiful scudding down the gray bay. But Judy thought the one with the big blue "3" on its sail was the best of all. That was because its name was *Judy,* too, and it was her father's boat.

"The *Judy* is out in front!" she squealed.

But Billy Ames and Stevie weren't listening to her. They were too busy talking about sailing. They talked about tacking and reefing and sailing into the eye of the wind.

Billy said, "Golly, Stevie, in two years I can help sail my father's boat!"

"I'm going next year," said Stevie. "Next year I'll help sail in the big race. Golly!"

Judy shouted, "Golly, Billy! Golly, Stevie! The *Judy* is still out in front!"

But they just nodded and went on talking.

Judy kicked at the green, slippery moss on the jetty. She tugged at Billy's pocket.

"I'm going this year," she said in a loud voice. "I'm going to help in the big race this year!"

Billy and Stevie both looked at her in surprise.

"You're never!" cried Billy.

Stevie said, "You're only six!"

Judy tossed her head. "Just the same, I'm going!" she said.

Her heart began to bump so hard she couldn't stand still. Judy knew her father hadn't said she could go. She knew she had better say, "I was only fooling," right away.

But Billy and Stevie looked at her as if she were just as big as they were.

"Are you, honest-to-goodness?" they asked.

Judy crossed her fingers inside the pockets of her dungarees. She nodded her head. Then she ran down the slippery jetty and back home as fast as she could go.

That night she tried to ask her father if she could go on the race. But her father looked very big and stern with his tanned face and bright blue eyes. Besides, he was busy talking to her mother. He was talking about tacking and reefing and sailing into the eye of the wind.

Sailing was all he talked about for days and days. Whenever Judy tried to ask if she could go along, he said, "Don't interrupt, Judy." Or else Mother said, "Judy, you mustn't talk when your mouth is full!"

And whenever Judy tried to tell Billy Ames and Stevie that she wasn't really going, the words would not quite come out.

At last it was the day before the race. Judy climbed down on her father's boat while it was tied to the dock. She ran her hands over the hot, shiny deck, and felt the warm, coarse canvas sails. Then she sat cross-legged in the cockpit and pretended.

"Now, it's tomorrow," Judy told herself. "Now the race is going to start. And I'm going along—"

She opened the little doors into the rope locker. There were coils of rope in there under the deck. But there was lots of room besides.

"Room enough for me to stow away!" whispered Judy.

She thought she could hide in there early in the morning and be there during the race.

"When the race is over," she thought, "I could crawl out and hop up on the dock. And then Billy and Stevie would see that I really truly did go along!"

Just before supper, Judy hurried down to the sailboat again. She put a pillow in the rope locker, and a box of crackers. She put a bottle of lime soda in the middle of a coil of rope. Then she put her lucky rabbit's foot under the pillow.

"Now the *Judy* is sure to win the race," she whispered.

And just after she had backed out of the rope locker, her father came down to the boat.

"Mother wants you to set the table, Judy," he said.

Judy ran home. She set the table and washed her face and hands. She never interrupted once when her father was talking. And right after supper, Judy said good night.

"Don't you feel well, Judy?" her mother asked.

Her father didn't say anything. He looked the way he always did when he was going to tell a joke. But he didn't tell one.

He just said, "Judy has a lot on her mind." Then he said, "Good night, Judy."

Judy was curled up in bed before it was nearly dark. She closed her eyes and listened to the water sloshing against the jetty. The sailboats were all rocking on the bay, now. Their sails were folded. They were rocking and waiting for tomorrow's race.

"If only I can wake up early enough," Judy whispered. In two minutes she was sound asleep.

When she woke up, it was so early that nobody else was awake. Judy scrambled out of bed, dressed in a wink, fixed her own breakfast, and tiptoed down to the dock.

She crawled into her stowaway place and pulled the doors closed—all but a tiny crack.

The waves lapped against the bottom of the boat and sounded nice and cool. But the sunshine beat down on the deck. Judy's hiding place got hotter and hotter. It smelled tarry from the rope. And Judy heard a tiny crackling noise that sounded like a mouse nibbling at her crackers.

She began to think her father would never come.

And just as she thought that, he jumped down into the boat. It seemed to rock much more wildly under the deck than it ever did on top! Suppose, just suppose, the *Judy* turned over in the race?

Now Judy didn't want to be a stowaway any more. She wanted to crawl out of the dark, hot little locker, and away from that much-too-close mouse. But she remembered Billy Ames and Stevie. She lay perfectly still and closed her eyes.

"I'll stand it somehow," she told herself.

And then her father said, "All right, Judy, come out of there. I intended taking you along all the time—"

Judy poked her head out of the little door. Her mouth made a surprised O.

And her father, who was busy raising the sail, said, "Bring the crackers and the soda and the pillow and the rabbit's foot with you."

Judy gulped. "How did you know they were here, Daddy?" she asked. "How did you know I was stowing away?"

"A bird told me," her father said. "A hungry seagull."

He laughed as if he had told a dandy joke.

"The same bird told me that we're going to win this race, sailor," he said.

Just then the wind filled the sails. The *Judy* skimmed over the bright blue bay toward the starting line.

The racing course was miles long. All morning the sailboats sailed around and around the course. The *Judy* seemed to go faster and faster and faster. When the race was over, the *Judy* had won. She won the big silver cup for being the fastest sailboat of all. And when at last Judy herself climbed out on her own dock, she had that splendid shiny prize in her two hands.

Stevie and Billy stared and stared at the cup. They said, "Golly, Judy!" over and over again. And they looked at Judy as if she were bigger than they were—and smarter than they were—and a real sailor, besides.

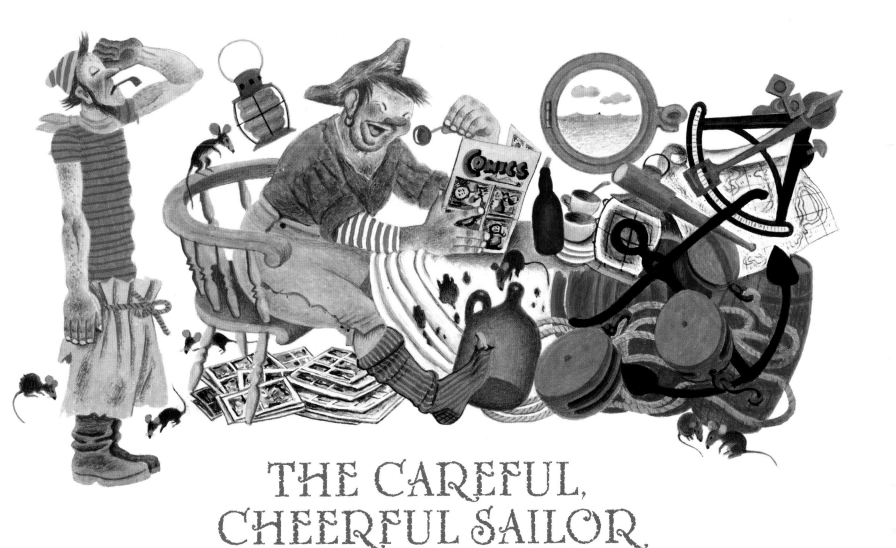

THE CAREFUL, CHEERFUL SAILOR

Once there was a careless ship that sailed carelessly with its sails full of holes and its hold full of rats. Nobody knew what the cargo was. If you asked the captain, he said, "I don't know. I didn't notice," and went back to reading his comic books.

But the cargo was heavy and the ship had a list. It leaned way over sideways, and when the sea was rough it leaned over so far that the waves washed the decks with sudsy foam. That was just as well because the sailors never had washed the decks and never would.

Even if the captain had looked up from his comic books long enough to say, "Sailors, ho! Wash the decks!" the sailors would have said:

"No, we don't want to wash the decks. We don't care if they are dirty."

And nobody knew where the careless ship was going. Nobody cared. Even if you had asked the pilot where it was going, he'd have scratched his head and said:

"I forget. Maybe we're going to latitude and maybe we're going to longitude. I don't care where we go, anyway."

He never went near the helm and never looked at the North Star or shot the sun, which was very careless in a pilot.

All he did was wish he were back in London eating sugar buns with currants.

But there was one careful sailor on the careless ship. He had a dreadful, busy time but he was always cheerful, nonetheless.

He mended sails until his thumb was numb.

And he spliced ropes until all the ropes were spliced into one rope.

He looked at the North Star every night.

And he shot the sun every single day.

He went to the helm at lunch hour and turned the wheel until the ship *looked* as if she were going some place, anyway.

He washed the dishes in the galley.

And he made a trap to catch the rats. It wasn't a very good trap for rats but it did catch the second mate when he went in the hold to steal some jam.

And whenever he sat down, that one careful sailor always sat on the high side of the listing ship to try and weigh it down even with the low side.

But one careful sailor can't take care of a careless ship. Oh, no—it takes a whole crew to keep a ship in shape.

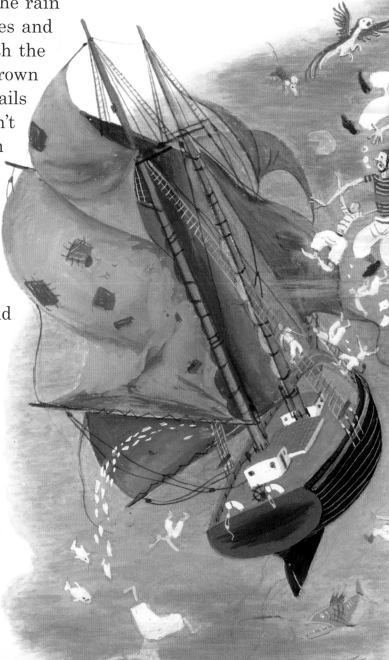

So one day, when a storm blew up and the rain rained in sheets and the wind blew in furies and the sea rose up and down like a whale with the whooping cough, the careless ship was thrown up in the thick gray air. It came down sails down. It rolled over full of water and it couldn't right itself because of the list, and so down it went, down and down into the slate-gray sea.

Bubbles came up . . . bubbles and bubbles.

And the captain came up with his comic books, and the pilot came up with his "I don't care," and the first mate and the second mate and all the careless crew.

They tried to swim but the waves were very rough. And they saw the one careful sailor in a neat lifeboat, rowing away with two neat oars. He had a tin of dry biscuits and a keg of clear water and every chance of reaching the mainland or at least an island of some sort.

But all the careless sailors and the captain and both mates climbed into the lifeboat.

It went down—
        And down—
                And down—
until all you could see was a lot of frowsy heads, and one tidy head, bobbing in the rough sea.

They bobbed for quite a while.

A seagull came and said, "My goodness, this is dangerous!"

And a porpoise came and said, "What's dangerous about it?"

And when everybody was very tired of bobbing, a ship sailed up.

It was a tidy ship, with a careful captain who liked everything shipshape.

He saw the bobbing heads through his well-polished spyglass and he slapped the gleaming rail and cried:

"Man the lifeboats!"

The crew knew their duty. They let down the boats and rowed out to the bobbing heads. They pulled the careless captain and careless crew out of the sea.

And the one careful sailor climbed out himself.

But when the bos'n of the careful ship saw that careless crew, he threw up his hands.

He looked at the careless captain and his wet comic books and he said, "Tut, tut, we can't rescue him! He bites his nails and our captain can't abide nails that are bitten!"

So he threw the captain, comic books and all, back into the sea.

And he couldn't save the pilot with his tousled hair.

Over went the pilot.

One by one the tidy bos'n observed the careless crew.

"None of them will do!" he declared. "Too careless. Holes in socks, showing toeses. Dirty faces, runny noses. Missing buttons, dirty nails! We never could clean them. We haven't the pails for a job like that!"

He looked very sorry but he said, "Throw them back!"

All the careless crew went back— "Splash!"—into the sea.

"What about me?" asked the one careful sailor with his cheerful smile.

The bos'n grinned a friendly grin and clasped the sailor's nice clean hand.

"You're just the man we want," said he. "Our captain will be glad to see such a tidy, shipshape sailor."

The captain was. He beamed with pleasure when he saw the sailor.

"This ship needs a careful mate. I fancy you will do first-rate—you tidy, careful sailor."

And the tidy sailor came to be the Admiral of the King's Navy—after several years, of course, and after many sailings and many scrubbing decks and many polishing railings.

He wears a neat three-cornered hat with ostrich feathers pressed out flat and a long blue coat with golden braid.

He's a splendid figure on parade.

That careful, cheerful sailor!

PIRATES' GLEN

Go shouting up the cobbled hill
    But whisper in the glen—
You never know when you may meet
    A band of pirate men!

It's true. They came here long ago
    With chests of pirate stuff.
You never know what we may find
    If we dig deep enough.

We might find ropes of oyster pearls
    Or heaps of gold doubloons,
Or gold from Madagascar, or
    A chest of silver spoons.

Or maybe ancient treasure maps
    Or diamonds by the ton,
Or cutlasses with jeweled hilts
    Or—just a skeleton!

Or—just around that darkish tree—
    Did you hear something crack?
The pirates might be coming now
    To get their treasure back!

Let's hurry up the ferny hill
    And not come back again.
I don't believe I want to meet
    A band of pirate men!

OLD CAPTAIN GARRETT

Old Captain Garrett of Peabody Lane
Walked with a limp, and he walked with a cane,

And he walked up the beach by the light of the moon
With a shovel all smooth at the tip, like a spoon.

He dug in the sand with great vigor and pleasure,
And said he was digging for lost pirate treasure.

All the people in town heard him say it. They said:
"Poor old Captain Garrett's not right in the head!"

But once on an evening quite foggy and drear,
Why, old Captain Garrett, he cheered a great cheer.

"I've found it!" he cried. "The lost treasure I sought!
And I've doubloons all golden, for things to be bought!"

He went shopping next day for wonderful things:
Scarlet coat, and a sash, and big golden earrings,

And a sword, and a knife, and a black pirate hat.
And he paid for them all with his treasure—like that!

Oh, he made a strange sight as he strutted about
With his limp and his sword and his loud pirate shout,

And his queer pirate clothes, and his bags full of gold.
But the people in town (so the story is told)

Bowed and smiled as he passed.
And they asked him to tea.

They said, "Captain Garrett's as smart as can be!"

THE WONDERFUL BOTTLE

Once there was a little girl who went to the seashore for the first time. She stayed there all summer long, and that was a wonderful summer.

On sunshiny days the little girl played at the edge of the sea. She paddled her feet in the little waves, and when they ran out, she looked to see what they had brought to shore.

They brought seaweed that popped when you pinched it, and strange shells and beautiful shells, and starfish that were hard as stone when you let them dry in the sun.

And on rainy days the little girl put on her boots and put up her umbrella and went for a walk up the cobbled hill. Halfway up she turned around and looked down at the harbor. It was full of ships that rocked and swayed in the rainy wind on the wet sea.

Then she went on, up and up the steep hill. And at the very top of the hill there was a small shop. The little girl stopped there and looked and looked and looked in the window.

That window was only as wide as the little girl was high, but it was full of the most wonderful things. There were small figures carved of wood: sailors and whales and a splendid sea serpent, and a bold pirate with one peg leg. There were conch shells that gave back the sound of the sea, and there were starfish.

And then there were ships.

The ships were tiny, but they looked just like the real ships in the harbor.

Some were on small wooden stands, and one, the most beautiful ship of all, was in a bottle. How it ever had gotten in, the little girl could not tell. The neck of the bottle was much too small for it to pass through.

She wanted very much to go into the shop and ask about that ship. But the old sailor inside never looked up. He had a stern and lonesome look, and he always seemed very busy. He was whittling away, and if you went in he might say, "Go away, little girl. I'm busy. Can't you see how busy I am, little girl?"

So the little girl did not go in.

She just stood outside in the drip-drip-drip of the rain and looked at the wonderful bottle. And then one day in the middle of the summer, this little girl was far up the beach watching sandpipers, watching sand cobblers, and she saw something bobbing in the shallow water. In she went—and out she came with a bottle in her two hands. It was a long bottle, flat on one side. It was as clear and green as a wave breaking in the sunshine. And it was a wonderful bottle just like the one in the window of the shop.

Now the little girl did not wait for rain.

She went straight up the hill in the sunshine, up to the top.

A bell tinkled when she opened the door of the shop. And when she put the wonderful bottle on the counter, the old sailor looked at her and smiled.

He didn't say he was busy.

And he didn't say, "Go away, little girl."

What he said was, "This is a splendid bottle for putting a ship in!"

He began at once to make a little ship. He carved the hull just the size to go through the neck of the bottle, and he painted it dark, deep red.

That was all he did that day, and the little girl went home.

But the little girl went back the next day and the next. Every day for days and days the little girl watched the old sailor work. He carved tiny masts and cut tiny sails. He made tiny ropes and ladders of linen thread. He painted all the parts with clear paint that was shiny.

It took a long time to finish that little ship.

And at last the day came when the little girl had to go back to the city.

She went to the beach and said good-bye to the seagulls and the starfish and the strange shells and the beautiful shells and the seaweed that popped when you pinched it.

And then she went up the cobbled hill to say good-bye to the old sailor and the wonderful bottle and the little ship that was not quite finished.

But when she went into the shop, the old sailor held up the ship with its folded sails.

"Now we'll put her in the bottle," he said.

He pushed the little ship through the neck of the bottle, right to the middle. Then he pulled on the threads that were looped about the masts.

Up they went—masts, sails, ropes, and all—and there was the ship all finished. There it was inside the bottle, and looking too big to have gone in!

The sails seemed full of wind, just as if the ship were sailing on a real sea. And the little girl saw that there really was water in the bottle.

She sniffed, and the water smelled salty like the sea.

She shook it a little, and the salt seawater tossed in tiny waves.

"It's the most wonderful bottle, and the most wonderful ship in the whole wide world," the little girl said.

And then it was time for her to go.

She thanked the old sailor for letting her watch, and hurried to the door.

But the old sailor called her back.

"Aren't you going to take your bottle, little girl?" he asked.

The little girl leaned way forward.

"With the ship inside?" she whispered.

"With the ship inside," said the old sailor.

He put the wonderful bottle in her hands.

He said it was hers to take back to the city.

Then he began to whittle away, and he would not look up when the little girl thanked him. He would not look up when she went out the door and the bell tinkled. He would not look up so she could wave good-bye. He just sat in his little shop whittling away, and the little girl went down the hill.

She took her bottle home to the house by the sea—

and home to her apartment in the city.

She put it on the windowsill in her own high-up room. And there it is every morning when the little girl wakes up. A tiny ship, in a wonderful sea-green bottle, sailing on a real little sea.

So the little girl never did say good-bye to the most wonderful part of that wonderful summer, after all.

ORDERS IS ORDERS

Once there was a little boy who lived with his aunt in a little house close to the sea. The white sand was in front of his house, with tufts of tough grass in it, and in front of the sand was the ocean. At first the ocean was shallow with flat little waves that spread out of the sand. Then it grew deeper with splashing waves that had white, sudsy foam on top. It grew deeper and deeper until it was so deep that nobody knew how deep it was, except one old whale and one or two sailors on the big ships out on the deep sea.

The little boy watched those big ships while his aunt gathered cockles and mussels alive, alive-o.

He thought he would like to be a sailor on a big ship. And he watched the ships so hard, and thought about being a sailor so hard, that when his aunt said, "Briny, lad, help me gather cockles and mussels alive, alive-o," he only half heard her.

That made his aunt shake her head.

One day, when she was shaking her head and gathering cockles and mussels alive, alive-o, the little boy went up to the little attic of the little house. He found an old trunk in the attic.

In it there was a fine sailor's spyglass that needed polishing—

a jacket and trousers that needed new buttons—

a sailor's hat that wanted a new ribbon—

and a sailor's log, which is not a log at all, but a book in which sailors write down what they do each day.

The little boy polished the sailor's spyglass, and sewed buttons on the sailor's suit, and put new ribbon on the sailor's hat. He wrote his name in the sailor's log.

Then he tried on all the sailor's clothes. They were quite too big for him, but he wore them just the same.

"Aunt," he said to his aunt, "I'm off to be a sailor."

His aunt stopped shaking her head and nodded it instead.

"Aye, lad," she said, "I thought you would soon be doing that."

She went back to gathering cockles and mussels alive, alive-o, and the little boy walked straight to the harbor and the biggest ship in the harbor. It was a long walk.

He asked to see the captain.

"Well, lad," said the captain, "what can I do for you?"

The little boy said, "I have a polished spyglass, a sailor's coat with buttons, a sailor's hat with a new ribbon, and a sailor's log with my name on it. Now, what I want is to be a sailor."

The captain looked very serious about being a sailor.

"Do you know how to obey orders?" he asked.

"What is that, please, sir?" asked the little boy.

"It's doing just exactly what you are told to do," the captain told him. "Do you do that?"

Now the little boy thought. He thought he would like to say "Yes" but he knew he could not. He knew he never did obey orders when his aunt said, "Briny, lad, help me gather cockles and mussels alive, alive-o."

So he said, "No, sir. I don't."

The captain looked stern. "Well, then," he said, "you certainly can't be a sailor on my ship."

The little boy gulped. He took out his sailor's log with his name in it.

"Please, sir," he said, "if you'll give me your name and address I will put it in my log book. Then when I learn to obey orders, I will come to see you again."

"Fine," said the captain with a smile, "fine. But remember, one order isn't orders. Two orders aren't orders, either. You take orders until your sailor's suit and sailor's hat fit just right. Then come to see me."

He gave the little boy his name and address. It was Captain Josiah Retort on board H.M.S. *Fearless*. The little boy wrote that in his log book.

Then he went home. That was a very long walk.

He put his sailor's spyglass and his sailor's suit and his sailor's hat back in the old trunk in the attic. But he kept his sailor's log under his arm.

Down to the beach he went, to find his aunt. She was very busy gathering cockles and mussels alive, alive-o.

"Briny, lad," she said, "help me gather cockles and mussels alive, alive-o."

"Yes, ma'am!" said the little boy.

He set right to work and gathered lots of cockles and mussels.

They tasted very good for supper in a sort of stew in a deep, green bowl.

And that night, before the little boy went to bed in his bed near a window where he could hear the big waves breaking into little waves and the big ship's horns telling each other where they were, he wrote in his log.

"Obeyed orders," he wrote.

He wrote that in his book every night until he was so big that his sailor suit with buttons and his sailor hat with a new ribbon fit him just right.

Then he took his spyglass and his log book and went back to see Captain Josiah Retort on board H.M.S. *Fearless*.

The captain looked in the log book full of "obeyed orders." He smiled. He shook the little boy's hand and said, "Now you may be a sailor on my ship!"

A sailor's life suited the little boy to a T.

He climbed up riggings—

and polished brass—

and battened down hatches.

He obeyed orders as fast as they were given.

He saw storms and strange foreign lands and he even saw the one big whale that knew how deep the ocean was.

"That is something worth writing in my log book," he said to himself. So he did. He wrote about seeing the whale on page 762.

He wrote about it to his aunt, too.

She was very pleased to get that letter.

She read it twice upside down and three times upside up. It seemed to make better sense that way. Then she put the letter in her pocket and patted it.

And then she went back to gathering cockles and mussels alive, alive-o.

SEAFARING TOMMY

Tommy's a seaman on cleaning-house day.
    With a mop and some soap and a pail,
He swabs the front porch, and the steps to the yard
    Till they shine like the back of a whale.

Tommy's a captain on washing-clothes day.
    When the wash blows out white on the line,
He sails in a basket just under the sheets,
    For sailing on Monday is fine.

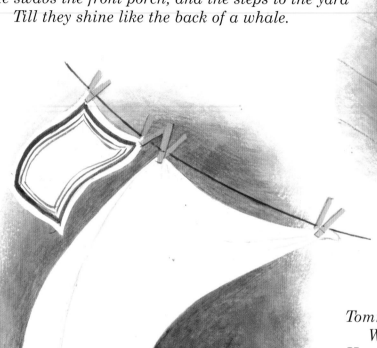

Tommy's a pirate on baking-things day.
    When warm cookies are piled on a plate,
He creeps down the stairs where the shadows are deep
    And he takes some for pieces of eight!

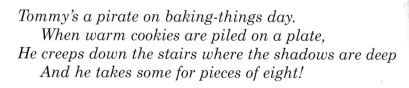

THE FLYING DUTCHMAN

Old Captain Garrett liked very much to tell stories. He told about storms and whales and desert islands. And do you know, in every story he ever told, he was swallowed whole, or drowned dead, or cooked to a crisp in the hot sun!

A very wonderful man he was, and all the children on the beach listened to his tales with open mouths.

"Did I ever tell you about me and the *Flying Dutchman*?" he asked one day.

The children shook their heads and came close.

"Well, sir," said Captain Garrett, "I'll tell you right now . . ."

And this was his story:

It was a fine day, so fine that I had to whistle at my work. I was a young man then, very brave and marvelous, and a capable second mate.

I said to the first mate, "Well, sir, fine weather behind us, fine weather ahead of us. A prosperous voyage, and we'll be home on time or my name's not Garrett."

The first mate straightaway clapped his hand over my mouth.

"Man!" he cried. "That's no way to talk. Your boasting's enough to tempt the *Flying Dutchman* to pursue us!"

Now, I had heard tell of the *Flying Dutchman*. A ghost ship, she was supposed to be. Aye. The story went that she would come at a ship head on—and if the ship turned so it wouldn't hit her, why, it would surely be wrecked on rocks or reefs.

But I took no stock in the tale. A ghost ship! Who would believe such nonsense?

35

I laughed it off with a hearty "Ho, ho, ho!"

But even as I laughed, the blue sky went black! A terrible storm came on us, sighing and roaring. Rain poured down like a wet wall, and our good ship tossed like a matchstick.

"See what you've done, man!" the first mate shouted.

And no sooner had he said that than the storm stopped as if it had never been. No wind blew. There was no sound on all the sea. But a heavy white fog hung about us, thick and wooly. I could scarcely see my own hand. Then suddenly, out of the silence, a fog horn sounded.

It set me shivering, I can tell you!

"Ship ahead!" whispered the first mate, and he swung the wheel to port.

Whooooooooooo! Whooooooooooooo!

The horn sounded to port!

Again the first mate swung the wheel. Again and again he turned the ship. But no matter what way he turned, the horn sounded just ahead.

Suddenly the fog lifted for a moment. Straight toward our bow came a great dark ship. She seemed to swoop down on us, and on her bridge stood a strange, pale captain. He pointed one bony finger right toward me!

"It's the *Flying Dutchman*!" the first mate hissed. "You tempted her with your boasting! Now we'll all perish on some fearsome rocks!"

Closer and closer came the wild dark ship. The first mate made to turn the wheel. But I put my hand on his arm.

"Sail straight at her," I begged.

Then I ran down from the bridge and hurled myself into the sea. Down I went, deep, deep, into the dark water, never to come up again.

And even as I did, the fog disappeared. The sky and sea were fair and blue. The *Flying Dutchman* was gone. But on each side of our good ship loomed jagged rocks. Another turn of the wheel and she would have crashed into them and sunk!

"Alas for the man who gave his life to save our ship!" sighed the first mate. "Alas for poor, brave, wonderful and marvelous second mate Garrett!"

Oh, all my shipmates grieved that I had drowned to satisfy the *Flying Dutchman*! But I never regretted it, nor do I to this day.

Now old Captain Garrett looked out to sea with a dreaming look that meant he would tell no more stories that day. And the children ran off to play at the edge of the sparkling sea in which the wonderful, brave, and marvelous captain had drowned so many times!

TWENTY-FIVE SAILORS

1. *Twenty-five sailors went down to the sea.*
   One was the first mate. "Look lively!" said he.

2. *Two stowed the cargo down deep in the hold*
   And battened down hatches to keep out the cold.

5. *Five lighted lanterns, the red and the green,*
   And swabbed till the decks were all shining
      and clean.

6. *Four shoveled coal in the furnace of steel.*

9. *One was the captain—he tried the lifeboats*
   And looked at the buttons on twenty-four coats.

10. *Then* toot! *went the whistle.*
    Ding dong! went the bell.

WENT DOWN TO THE SEA

3. *Three stored provisions to eat day by day.*

4. *Four made the bunks in a seamanlike way.*

7. *Three charted courses and tried out the wheel.*

8. *Two called the hour out, "Eight bells!*
   Time to go!"
   And pulled up the anchor with "Yo-ho-ho-ho!"

11. *Up the stack went the smoke with a fine*
    sooty smell.

12. *Out of the harbor, and out of the bay*
    The ship it went sailing away and away.

And twenty-five sailors, as proud as could be, Twenty-five sailors went sailing to sea.

THE RESCUE OF THE SEA COW

Tommy and Jimmy lived in a lighthouse out on the deep blue bay. In the daytime they watched the ships go sailing by, and they played games on the salty rocks, and they watched their father clean the lamps in the top of the lighthouse tower. At night they listened to the waves and the bell buoys and the sound of the ship's horns.

Some ships whistled. Some hooted like old, old owls, and one had a deep, long horn that sounded like a cow saying moooooo.

The two little boys called that ship the *Sea Cow*. They liked that ship with the deep, long horn sound.

"I wish we knew which ship she was," they whispered to each other in the night in their round room in the lighthouse.

But they never could tell. Not ever.

When the ships went sailing by in the day, they did not blow their horns, unless it was foggy. And when it was foggy, Tommy and Jimmy could not see the ships at all.

One day it was sunny. The sky was high and blue, and everybody felt so good at breakfast that the lighthouse keeper laughed out loud.

"Mother," he said to his wife, "I'm going out to oil the bell buoys so they won't get rusty. You come along and bring your fishing line. It just might be that you'll catch a bluefish. Then we'll eat bluefish with lemon and butter for supper and a pie of canned blueberries."

The little boys' mother said, "Well, I don't know. What if a storm should blow up? What if a fog should blow in? Who would light the lamps so the ships would beware the rocks?"

The lighthouse keeper looked up at the blue sky. He thought of the bluefish and the blueberry pie and said:

"Tommy and Jimmy can be lighthouse keepers for today."

That made the little boys feel proud. They felt proud when their mother and father rowed away from the rocky island. And when the rowboat was only a speck on the blue bay, they felt very proud.

"We're the lighthouse keepers now," they said, and they didn't play on the rocks that day. They had to be sure everything on the island was just right. They looked in the rocky caves to be sure no pirates had come ashore in the night. They fed the seagulls the breakfast scraps. And they dusted all the rooms clean as a whistle, so there would be no dust to dim the lamps in the lighthouse tower.

Then they went outdoors again. They looked up at the sky. It wasn't blue anymore. It was gray and thick.

The bay and the sea were gray, too. And a splendid big steamer was coming into the gray bay. Their father rowed up close to it. He seemed to be talking to an officer on the splendid ship. Then he sat down and rowed his boat back toward the rocky island just as fast as he could row.

But when his boat was halfway back, it disappeared! A fog had drifted in from the sea, a fog as heavy as a gray blanket. Then everything was still, except the bells on the bell buoys. They rang softly through the heavy gray fog.

"Halloooo!" called their father.

Tommy and Jimmy called, "Halloooo!" But their father could not quite tell where the island was. The bells seemed to ring everywhere, and the two little boys' halloo seemed everywhere, too.

Just then the little boys heard a deep moooooo, out on the foggy bay. It sounded near and far away both at once, and it sounded all around.

"It's the *Sea Cow*!" cried Tommy.

And Jimmy shouted, "Come on!"

Both boys ran into the lighthouse, and wisps of fog slipped in with them. They ran up and up and up the winding stairs into the high-up tower. Tommy climbed up to the lighthouse lamps, and Jimmy handed up the matches and the lighter.

"Hurry," he whispered. Tommy lit all twelve lamps just as fast as he could.

When they were all lit, the great light shone out the windows. It shone out through the fog.

And the *Sea Cow,* much too close to the rocks, blew its deep mooing horn and turned just in time. A minute later it would have been wrecked!

Now the boys' father saw the light and rowed straight toward it. Soon father and mother had landed at the foot of the lighthouse.

"You were good lighthouse keepers," the father told the two little boys at supper. He gave them each a big piece of bluefish and a bigger piece of blueberry pie. And after supper they went to sleep in their round room in the lighthouse, with the waves and the fog and the bell buoys all around and the light streaming across the bay.

In the morning the fog was gone and the sky was blue. The splendid steamer that the little boys had seen the day before came steaming toward the rocky island. It was gleaming white, and had lots of flags, and a name in gold letters on the bow.

The name was *The Queen of Columbia.*

But all at once that splendid ship blew her horn. And it sounded deep and long and low like a cow's moo.

"It's the *Sea Cow!*" whispered Tommy and Jimmy both together.

42

And then that splendid steamer dropped her anchor. An officer with gold braid on his blue coat got into a small boat. Two sailors rowed him across to the rocky island. He climbed ashore and shook hands with Tommy. He shook hands with Jimmy.

"You saved my ship from the rocks yesterday," said the officer. "I came to thank you."

He gave them a long package, shook hands again, and went back to the ship.

In that package there were flags—four beautiful bright signal flags. Two were for Tommy and two were for Jimmy.

Their father showed them how to signal words to the ships.

And ever after that, there was fun whenever *The Queen of Columbia* steamed across the bay. The boys, waving their signal flags, "talked" with the officer in gold braid on the bridge.

THE STUBBORN, STUBBORN SAILOR

(Suggested by Irene Alleman)

Now once there was a sailor who
    Was very tall and thin.
He always wore a raincoat and
    He always wore a grin.
He always was found sitting
    In the still and sunny spots,
A-trying hard as he could try
    To tie the sailor knots.

He said, "I'll tie a bowline, now,"
    And then, "I'll tie a reef . . .
A mooring knot . . . a half-hitch—so!"
    But always came to grief.
For all his knots were knotted to
    His whiskers or his hair.
(When shipmates tried to show him how,
    He said, "Shucks! I don't care!")

One day when it was foggy, all
    Around the rocking ship,
He sat there tying knots, and sighing—
    "These knots—they seem to slip!"
And when the cook called, "Chow time—chow!"
    A-banging on his pots,
The sailor came with dolphin-leaps—
    He'd tied himself in knots!

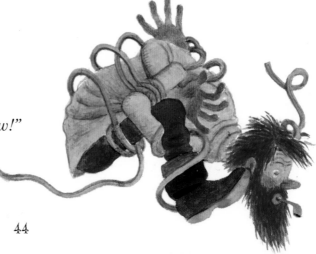

44

THE ICEBOUND SHIP

"Icebergs ahead!" shouted one sailor.

"Icebergs astern!" shouted another.

"Icebergs to port!" the first mate cried.

"Icebergs to lee!" shouted the crow's-nest watch.

"Icebergs everywhere!" thought the captain, rubbing his cold hands. "What to do! What to do!" he muttered, and he paced up and down the icy deck.

Then he shouted, "Sail between those two icebergs!" He pointed ahead at two mountains of ice far enough apart for the ship to sail through.

The ship sailed toward them. It sailed between them. And there it was, with a great iceberg on each side.

Suddenly, one iceberg started to get smaller—and the other iceberg began to get bigger!

"Ice is shifting!" shouted the crow's-nest watch.

"Full steam ahead!" the captain cried.

"Aye, aye, sir!" cried the engineer.

But it was too late. Those two ice peaks were part of one enormous iceberg with a shelf in the middle. Before the ship could pass, the shelf rose up from the sea—and the ship was sailing in an icy lake with towering cliffs of ice all around.

"We're trapped!" the crow's-nest watch called.

"We're lost!" cried a sailor.

"We'll freeze!" the cook wailed, waving a pot.

"Or worse—" whispered an old sailor who thought he heard a rumbling.

In a moment, everyone heard the rumbling. Everyone heard an icy groaning and crunching—and then, with a tremendous loud *CRACK!* the ice shelf split right in two!

Cold green waves splashed up. Spray splashed up and froze the moment it hit the rigging. The ship bounced and bobbed and rolled in a strip of sea between two ice cliffs.

"Full steam ahead!" the captain shouted.

The ship raced ahead between the frozen cliffs.

Out it went into the open sea. Just as it did, one cliff fell *CRASH!* into the other cliff. Chunks of ice spun through the air. The cold sea tossed in great waves.

"Due south!" cried the captain.

The ship turned south and headed home.

"We're saved!" the crow's-nest watch called out, and all the happy sailors shouted, "Hooray!"

THE BIG LITTLE
COOK'S BOY

The *Gallant Tar* was an enormous big four-masted schooner.

And all the sailors on the *Gallant Tar,* from the captain (who was six feet nine) to the cook (who was six feet one), were big tall men with mustaches.

But the cook's boy was not big.

He was a wee bit of a boy.

At first all the sailors looked way down at him and thought, "Avast! This wee bit of a boy is not big enough for our ship. We'll have to get a big boy in the next port."

The cook said it right out loud.

That made the cook's boy feel even smaller.

But the boy said to himself, "Great deeds make big men." That was something his mother had always told him. And he did his work as well as if he were six feet nine.

He peeled potatoes white and clean. He scoured pots until they shone, and worked his fingers to the bone keeping the galley shining. He set the tables for captain and crew, and never minded carrying stew to the men on watch when the sea was stormy.

47

Everybody on the *Gallant Tar* came to think that the cook's boy was a fine cook's boy.

"He's the best we *ever* had," they said.

And then, one dark and moonless night, a pirate ship slipped silently up alongside the *Gallant Tar*.

Twenty fierce pirates crept aboard.

They had knives in their teeth and pistols (the double-barrelled pirate kind) in their hands. They captured everybody on the *Gallant Tar* and lined them up on deck.

"Sailors," said the pirate captain, "I give you a choice. Either you can join the pirates and do just as I say—or I'll put you below IN CHAINS!"

All the sailors on the *Gallant Tar*, from the captain (six feet nine) to the cook (six feet one), said, "We are honest sailors, and we will NOT join the pirates and do as you say!"

But when it was time for the cook's boy to decide, he said to himself, "Below in chains I can't do any great deeds. Above and free, it may be that I can."

He said to the pirate captain, "I'll be a pirate." But he kept his fingers crossed as he said it.

Nobody noticed that. All the pirates cheered.

"Yo ho ho and a dead man's chest,
This cook's boy seems to know what's best!"

The sailors of the *Gallant Tar* scowled at the cook's boy. Then they walked by him on their way belowdecks and to their chains without even looking at him. And they mumbled in their mustaches, "This cook's boy is a coward! He's the worst cook's boy we ever had."

The cook's boy tried to pretend he didn't care. He tried very hard to pretend he was a real bad, bloodthirsty pirate. He did just as the pirate captain said. Before long all the pirates thought he *was* a real pirate.

They asked his advice about where to bury their treasure, and they let him decide who was the best knife thrower in the crew. They had him polish their guns and sharpen their knives, and they liked his cooking very much. And all the time the cook's boy was polishing or sharpening or cooking, he was trying to think up a brave plan for a great deed.

One night he thought up a plan.

The next morning he walked right up to the pirate captain.

"There's plenty of white chicken put down in fat in the ship's stores," he said, "and there's plenty of red wine in a moldy cask. Now, what I say is, why not let me cook an extra grand dinner to celebrate your capture of the *Gallant Tar*?"

The captain grinned a greedy grin.
"A capital idea!" he roared.
And the other pirates sang:

*"Yo ho ho and a dead man's chest,
This cabin boy sure knows what's best!"*

The cook's boy cooked a splendid meal. He even made baked beans and pies. And he filled the pirates' plates and cups again and again and again.

The pirates ate until they felt stuffed, and drank the red wine until they felt drowsy. When they all had their chins on their arms, and their arms on the table, the cook's boy brought in the pies.

"Wow!" said the pirate captain. "Wow!"

He cut the pies and passed big wedges all around. All that pie made the pirates sleepier than ever.

"It's time to take bread and water to the sailors in the chains below," said the cook's boy.

The pirate captain groaned. He was too stuffed to go below. He was too sleepy, too.

"You take it down," he said to the cook's boy. "Be sure to lock the door when you come out."

He gave his big key ring to the cook's boy. Then he put his head on the table and began to snore big pirate snores. All the other pirates put their heads down, too. And all twenty pirates snored—snore, snore, snore.

The cook's boy grinned.

He tiptoed all around the big table and took all the pirates' knives, and all their guns, which were the double-barrelled pirate kind.

He put them in a bag.

Then he slipped down below where all the sailors were in chains.

The sailors wouldn't even look at him.

But when the little cook's boy took out the key ring and unlocked all their chains—then they looked!

Their eyes were as round as the full moon. Their mouths were as round as portholes.

"Silence!" whispered the cook's boy. "Take off your boots and follow me up above. Quiet, now!"

He gave each big sailor a knife or a double-barrelled pirate gun, and he led them back to the sleeping pirates.

All the big sailors crept up on the pirates with their knives and guns ready.

"SNORE, SNORE, SNORE," went the pirates.

The sailors crept closer and closer, but still the pirates did not wake up.

"Pick them up," breathed the cook's boy, "and carry them below!"

And the big sailors picked up the twenty pirates. They carried them below and put them in chains. The cook's boy locked the locks and gave the key ring to his own captain, who was six feet nine.

Then his captain and all the sailors and the cook went up on deck. They set the *Gallant Tar* toward home, where the pirates would be put in jail.

The captain picked up the cook's boy and set him on his shoulders.

"Give three cheers for the cook's boy!" he said.

The sailors didn't need to be told twice. They threw up their caps and shouted, "Hip! Hip! HOORAY for the brave little cook's boy!"

They said, "He's the best little cook's boy we EVER had!"

And the cook's boy, up there on the captain's shoulders, was a good three feet higher than any of the big sailors on the *Gallant Tar,* from the captain, who was six feet nine, to the cook, who was six feet one.

He looked down and he smiled, and he thought to himself, "My mother was right when she said 'Great deeds make big men!'"

As for the pirates below in chains, all they said was: "SNORE, SNORE, SNORE!"

IN THE SEA AN OYSTER

In the sea an oyster
Makes a wondrous pearl,
And on the windy seashore
A ragged fisher girl
Wishes for a penny
To buy a sugar bun—
Wishes she had many.
(Pennies she had none.)
The sea turns and tosses
And tips the oyster bed,
And out rolls the oyster
Heels over head.
"Oh, what a pretty oyster!"
The fisher girl cries.
And when it is opened
She opens wide her eyes
And whispers and whispers,
"A king's ransom pearl!
I'll live like a princess,
A king's little girl!"

LIGHTHOUSE

A little boy who couldn't sleep
  Sat tall up in his bed
And watched the lighthouse flashing
  Way out at Lobsterhead.

"When I am grown I'll keep that light
  As bright as any star
To guide the ships to harbor
  From journeyings afar!

"I'll live out in the lighthouse there
  Alone up on the rocks
And signal for provisions
  To watchers on the docks.

"I'll fill the empty lanterns with
  The best sperm oil from the whales,
And I'll polish up the windows
  With salty sea in pails.

"I'll keep the beacon gleaming out
  Across the stormy sea,
And all the ships will curtsy
  When they sail clear of me!"

But way out in the lighthouse there
  The weary keeper said:
"Someday I shall be sleeping in
  A quiet village bed!

"Then I'll pull great velvet curtains
  Around my bed so tight
That I won't hear the surf pound
  Nor see the beacon light.

"I'll go walking on the cobbles,
  And dine so full and well
With the fine chatty townsmen, I'll
  Forget the whale oil smell!"

But all throughout the stormy night
  The beacon threw its beam
Across the boy's small bedstead
  And through the keeper's dream.

And all the weary sailor men
  Steered wide of Lobsterhead
And its sharp rocks that jutted
  Up from the ocean bed.

LONG-AGO TOBY

This was all long ago.

Long ago, a little boy named Toby lived in a seafaring town. Almost all the fathers in the town were sailors. They went down to the sea in big sailing ships. And when they came back there was a great hubbub and hullabaloo. The whole town turned out to greet the sailors back from the sea.

But this one little boy named Toby had a father who was not a sailor. His father built big sailing ships.

And every night he came home to his little boy. He told Toby stories that began, "Once upon a time, when I was a sea captain. . . ." He took his little boy for walks along the shore. And he tucked his little boy in bed.

All that was fine. Toby and his father were the best of friends, long ago.

But one night when they were eating supper together, the father said, "I should like to go to sea on the fine big ship I'm building. . . ."

He said he would like to see the strange foreign places again. "I'd like to see the whales," he said, "and the flying fish. I'd like to feel the deck rolling under my feet."

Toby thought about his father going away.

He did not like it at all. Big tears popped into his eyes.

"Perhaps I could go with you?" he asked.

His father looked at the tears. "Toby is only a little boy," he thought. "Only a little boy with tears in his eyes."

"No, Toby," he said. "Little boys can't go to sea."

Then the big tears rolled down Toby's face. His father sighed a little and patted the boy's head.

"I'll stay ashore then," the father said. "Never mind, Toby. I'll stay ashore."

But, do you know, at night the father would stand outside in the garden. He would listen to the sound of the sea and sniff the salt smell. He would walk up and down the garden path, rolling a little, as if he were on a rolling deck.

Toby saw him do it, night after night, long ago. He thought of all the stories his father had told him about the wonderful life at sea. And all at once, he thought how much his father must want to be a sea captain again.

So the next day, Toby went up to the attic.

He took his father's captain's clothes out of a big sea chest. He asked Lucy Hawkins (who kept house for them) to air the clothes, and she did.

"Could you press them, too?" he asked.

Lucy Hawkins said yes, indeed she could. She pressed the big blue coat and the blue trousers. Then Toby put the captain's clothes on his father's bed.

And that night, when his father came home and saw the clothes, he didn't say a word.

His eyes twinkled at supper, but he still didn't say a word.

The little boy waited and waited for his father to say something. When he was too tired of waiting, he said, "If you see a whale when you go to sea, will you look at it very hard through your glass? Then you can tell me exactly how it looks."

Toby's father didn't answer that.

He said, "Who put my captain's clothes on my bed?"

And Toby said, "I did, sir. I wanted them to be all ready when your new ship is ready to go to sea."

He sat up straight and tall when he said it, and he smiled. Then Toby didn't look like a little boy at all.

"You're getting to be quite a big boy," said his father. He put down his napkin and stood up.

He took Toby up to the attic. There he opened a small sea chest. He took sailor clothes out of it and held them up. They were just the size for a little boy.

"These clothes were mine," the father said. "I wore them when I first went to sea."

"You were just my size!" whispered Toby.

His father nodded his head. Then he said, "Ask Lucy Hawkins to air them and press them, and put them on your bed. They'll be just the thing for you to wear when you go to sea with me."

Toby took the sailor clothes in both arms.

He smiled the happiest kind of smile and ran down the stairs, long ago.

And do you know, he rolled a little bit as if the stairs were rolling, too, on a ship at sea.

THE LITTLE LOST ISLAND

Once upon a time there was a little island. It was close by the side of a big island. When you looked from the big island, you could not see the little island because of the trees. And when you looked from the sea, you could not see the little island, either—because it looked like part of the big island.

But there it was just the same, a little island with a soft sand beach, and one palm tree, and a small thicket full of singing birds, and one monkey.

Yes, there was the little island, and nobody knew it was there.

And then, one day, a big pirate came rowing all around the big island. He was looking for a good place to hide and bury a big treasure chest full of treasure.

All at once, he came around the big island just right, close to the shore, and he saw the little island straight in front of him.

"Aha!" whispered the big pirate. "I'll hide and bury my treasure on this little island. No one will ever find it. No one will ever think I'd hide it on such a little island when there is a fine big island so close by!"

He dug a deep hole on the little island and buried his big treasure chest in the soft sand. And he rowed away laughing to himself. That big pirate was so sure he could find the little island any time he wanted to.

But he could not.

Years later, when he came back to get his treasure, he could not find the little island at all.

First he could not see it because of the trees in the way. Then he could not see it because it looked like part of the big island.

The big pirate did not find it ever after.

He rowed away, roaring with anger, and the big treasure chest stayed there on the little lost island, buried deep in the soft sand.

It stayed there for years and years and hundreds of years on the quiet little island that nobody saw and nobody found and nobody knew was there except the birds that sang and the one monkey (who was not the same monkey, but the great-great-great-great-grandchild of the one monkey who had been there when the pirate had buried his treasure chest).

And then, one day, a little boy and a little girl were playing on the big island. They walked all around the shore, near the edge, looking for a good place to have a picnic. And suddenly they saw the little island.

"Oh!" they said together.

The little boy put their lunch inside his shirt and rolled up his overalls. The little girl tucked up her skirt. And they both waded out to the little island.

They climbed the one palm tree.

And they ate their lunch on the soft sand in the sunshine.

They went around the beach looking for shells. The little girl listened to the singing birds, and once she thought she saw a small gray monkey peeping at her out of the thicket. Then the little boy, with his pockets full of shells, and the little girl, with her wondering about the monkey, waded back to the big island.

They went home for supper.

When it was dark, the little boy said, "I think there was treasure buried on that little island!"

The little girl said, "I think so, too. What will we do with the treasure when we dig it up?"

"I'll buy a real ship," said the little boy. "What will you buy?"

The little girl thought about the one monkey.

"I'll buy the whole little island!" she said at last.

And the next day, the little boy and the little girl looked for the little island again. They walked all around the big island. But when they looked from the shore, they couldn't see it because of the trees. And when they waded out and looked from the sea, they didn't see the little island because it looked like part of the big island.

They never did find the little island.

Not ever.

So there it still is, that little lost island, with its soft sand, and its one palm tree, and its thicket full of singing birds, and its one monkey, and the big treasure chest buried deep in its soft sand.

Nobody knows the treasure is there, and nobody knows the island is there, and nobody bought the island, and nobody owns the island.

So, if ever you happen to find it, all you need to do is put a flag on it and say, "I claim this little lost island for my own!"

And then it will be your island forever—
one palm tree
    soft sand
        singing birds
            small thicket
                one monkey
                    pirate treasure
                      AND ALL!

THE WHALE, THE WHALE

"Leave the salt sea to me!"
Says the whale.
Chase him—he'll break up your boats
With his tail.
Seek him—he'll hide
In the depths of the sea,
Deep in the shadowy, fathomless sea,
Down with the trembling anemone,
Down with the wrecks of ships
He'll hide.
Under the waves,
Under the tide,
"Deep in the dark salt sea!"
Says the whale.
"Leave it to me, the dark salt sea;
Leave the salt sea to me!"
Start for home and he'll rise again

Up to the surface,
Blowing his spout,
Rolling and lolling, big as a ship,
With a whale of a smile
On his whale of a lip!
Sing out, "She blows!"
And then look out—
He'll disappear with a flip of his tail.
"My terrible tail,"
Says the terrible whale.
And he may come up twenty miles away,
Or half a world,
Or a year and a day,
Or never again in the bright salt sea.
"It just might be,
You'll never see me again in the sea!"
Says the whale.

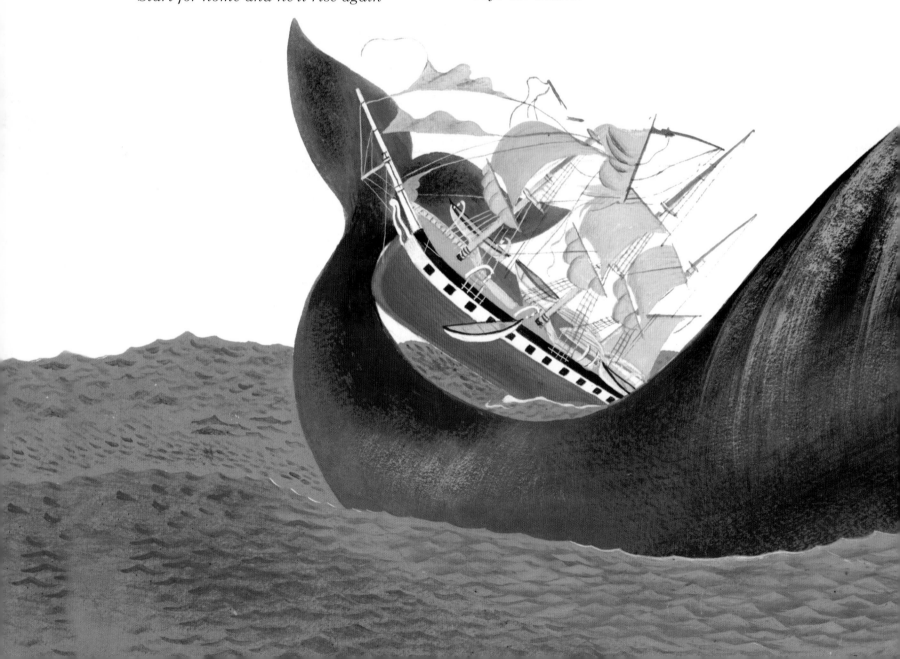

RAINY DAY SAILBOAT

Once upon a time there was a fine toy sailboat.

It was not a toy shop sailboat all painted red with a star on its sail. And it was not a shiny blue sailboat such as a little boy's daddy might make for him.

No. This was the kind of sailboat a little boy might make for himself on a rainy day. It was made of a block of wood, and a wooden lollipop stick, and a bit of cloth out of the scrap bag.

It was exactly that kind of sailboat.

And when the sun came out, the little boy said, "Now I'll see how my sailboat sails."

He put a nail in the front and tied a string to it. Then he ran, in his bare feet, down to the brook, which was deep and noisy after the rain.

The little boy put his sailboat in the water. It bobbed and danced. A small wind blew the sail, and *puff!* down the brook went that fine little sailboat.

Faster and faster it went.

Faster and faster and—*pop!* the nail popped right out of the front! Then the little sailboat went running away down the brook with the little boy after it.

It went around a rock, and it went under a fern that was dripping raindrops. It went over a fish that wasn't hungry and over a fish that was hungry, and under a bridge. Then it went around a bend, and when the little boy came to the bend, it was out of sight.

The little boy put the nail and string in his pocket. He gulped and said, "Well, anyway, my sailboat that I made sails like sixty."

He walked slowly home along the wet, squashy bank, wishing he had hammered the nail in a bit farther. When he got home, his mother said, "Supper is ready, and we'll eat as soon as your daddy comes home from fishing."

Just then the screen door banged.

The little boy's daddy came into the kitchen.

"Did you catch any fish?" the little boy asked.

"No, I didn't," said his daddy, "but I did catch something else in the brook."

He opened the lid of his creel, and the little boy looked in. In the creel there was a fine toy sailboat.

It was not the kind all painted red, and it was not the kind all painted blue. It was the kind of sailboat a little boy might make for himself on a rainy day. It was made of a block of wood, and a wooden lollipop stick, and a bit of cloth out of the scrap bag.

"It's just exactly my own sailboat that I lost!" said the little boy.

He pulled the string out of his pocket and hammered the nail into his sailboat. He hammered it all the way in, so it could never pop out. Then he put his sailboat on the table. He put it right beside his plate so he could look at it before and after every bite.

And the little boy's supper tasted very good and delicious on that day that had been raining and wasn't anymore.

THE SAD SEA-COOK

1. We were sailing, most serene-like,
    On an early morning course
When we heard a voice halloo us
    And the voice was sad and hoarse.
'Twas a thing most disconcerting,
    Aye, it gave us quite a shock
To observe a sea-cook sitting,
    Sighing sadly, on a rock.

3. "Mates," he sighed, "I never wanted
    To be anything at sea—
But they shanghaied me at midnight
    And they made a cook of me.
First they put me in the galley—
    Next they gave me books on cooking,
Then they said they'd be back later
    Just to see how lunch was looking.

2. "Cook," we called, "we'd gladly save you,
    But we know, as seamen oughter,
That a rock the size of that one
    Is much bigger under water.
And we daren't risk our vessel,
    Just to save you from the sea!"
Then the sea-cook told his story—
    It was sad as it could be.

4. "Well, I sat down by the cookstove
    In a darkish kind of nook
And I tried the best I knew how
    To start learning how to cook.
But I used a lot of pepper
    And it made them cough and sneeze
(For you always use up pepper
    When you can't read recipes!).

5. "And I tried a thing with apples
       And some onions, whole, as well—
But they didn't like the apples
       'Cause they had an onion smell.
And I tried a kind of pudding
       But it cooked up slippery wet—
Went a-skidding through the galley
       And they haven't caught it yet.

7. We had lately lost our own cook—
       So I thought I'd pull him in.
"We could give him easy cooking,"
       I kept thinking, "to begin.
I can set him washing dishes
       Or perhaps he can make tea."
So I set out in a dinghy
       For the sea-cook in the sea.
"Cook," I cried, "I'll try to save you
       (For your talk has touched my heart)
If you'll try to pick up cooking—
       Something easy for a start."

6. "Then the crew all lost their tempers,
       And the captain took his sword
And kept prodding at my backbone
       Till I hurried overboard.
It was far from any island,
       And I couldn't find a dock,
So at last I climbed to safety
       On this large and vacant rock."

8. But the sea-cook pulled his hair out,
       And he cried an awful cry—
"No! I'll never take up cooking,
       I would rather drown and die!
For I don't like level measures,
       And I hate to stir and whip—
And I'll never let you take me
       Back to cooking on a ship!"
So I turned back in my dinghy
       And my tears fell in my sock,
And I left the sea-cook sitting,
       Sighing sadly, on the rock.

SEA SERPENTS

Once upon a time sailors everywhere believed that there really were sea serpents.

"Oh, yes," the sailors told each other, "oh, yes, there are serpents in the sea, all right. Ninety feet long they are, with heads like dragons. They squirm and wriggle through the sea, snorting fire. And when they see a ship—slither, slither, slither—they wrap themselves around it. Pull and pull! They drag it down into the sea. Down into the dark deep they pull it, and it's never seen again."

"Sea serpents," they said. "Oh, yes. There are serpents slithering in the sea!"

All the sailors shivered.

They whispered to each other, "Did YOU ever see a sea serpent?"

"Oh, yes!"

"Oh, yes!"

"Oh, yes!" they all said.

"I saw a sea serpent once," said a tall, thin sailor. "Oh, a terrible creature it was, indeed. We sailed toward it, ready with our whale harpoon. And *zinnng!* we threw it. And *plish!* we got him. We pulled him in, that terrible sea serpent. But when we got him up on deck, why, that serpent had changed into a floating log—that was all!"

All the sailors nodded their heads.

"Oh, yes," they said. "There are sea serpents, all right."

And a short, stout sailor said his ship had been chased by a sea serpent.

"Oh, yes," he said. "Closer and closer it came, writhing and slithering, closer and closer. We put on full sail—but it still came closer. We shouted, 'Oh, help!' but it slithered up to our stern. We all looked down with eyes popping and hearts pounding—and it changed into a school of porpoises leaping in and out of the waves, one after another, single file!"

"Oh, yes," said all the sailors. "There are sea serpents, all right."

"Once," said an old sailor, "I saw a sea serpent, too. This one was two hundred feet long. It was shiny black, and smoke came out of its nose. When we came close, it looked sort of like rocks. When we came

closer, the smoke was coming from a fire. A sailor stood by the fire waving his shirt. 'I got marooned on those rocks!' he told us when we took him aboard. So the sea serpent had changed into a rocky reef—"

"Oh, yes," all the sailors agreed. "There are sea serpents, all right. What if they do always turn out to be logs, or fish, or rocky reefs? Haven't we seen them slithering and snorting with our own eyes?"

"Oh, yes," said all the sailors.

And they all nodded their heads and went right on believing in sea serpents for all they were worth.

SEAGULLS

When you see cloud-white seagulls
    Sailing up the bay,
They make you think of rolling seas
    And places far away,
Strange adventure places . . .
    And then you want to be
A free and roving sailor
    Sailing on the sea.
When sailormen spy seagulls
    Flying toward their bow,
They know it means they're close to land—
    That any minute now
They'll sail into harbor.
    And then they're glad to be
Back from a journey
    And home from the sea.

FOG HORNS

Sometimes at night when I'm in bed
   I pull the pillow round my head,
For fog horns on the big dark lake
   Cry out and keep me wide awake.
They take a breath and then they cry,
   With voices shrill or deep or high,
"W-H-H-H-O-O-O ARE YOU?"
   And "W-H-H-E-R-E AM I?"

But when I watch the lake by day,
   And all the fog has blown away,
And pilots on the lake can see,
   The ships move onward silently.
They look so proud and bold that I
   Can't quite believe I heard them cry,
"W-H-H-H-O-O-O ARE YOU?"
   And "W-H-H-E-R-E AM I?"